Timmy~

I know you will enjoy this book, I sure did. As you grow older you will understand the meaning behind it. Don't be sad when Jack and Bob are seperated. Just like real life. Everything works out. Sometimes you'll be happy. Both of those emotions are what make life worth living the book you'll hurt and other times and I know that as you grow up, I'll I love you, Timothy. Enjoy the book always be there if you need me. Take care & merry Christmas!

All my love~
Sister

Bob and Jack

Also by Jeff Moss
With Illustrations by Chris Demarest

THE BUTTERFLY JAR
THE OTHER SIDE OF THE DOOR

Bob and Jack

A Boy and His Yak

by
Jeff Moss

Illustrated by
Chris Demarest

BANTAM BOOKS

NEW YORK · TORONTO · LONDON · SYDNEY · AUCKLAND

BOB AND JACK
A Bantam Book / November 1992

Library of Congress number: 92-17458

ISBN 0-553-08931-5

Published simultaneously in the United States and Canada

Bantam Books are published by Bantam Books, a division of Bantam Double-
day Dell Publishing Group, Inc. Its trademark, consisting of the words "Bantam
Books" and the portrayal of a rooster, is Registered in U.S. Patent and Trade-
mark Office and in other countries. Marca Registrada. Bantam Books, 666
Fifth Avenue, New York, New York 10103.

PRINTED IN THE UNITED STATES OF AMERICA

RAN   0   9   8   7   6   5   4   3   2   1

For
Jonathan
and
Alexander

This is the story of a boy named Jack
Who more than anything wanted a yak.

Whenever his birthday or Christmas came,
The thing Jack wished for was always the same.

"A yak! A yak!" he begged his dad.
"I'll be good forever and I'll never be bad."

"A yak! A yak!" he begged his mama.
"It's better than a puppy or a goldfish or a llama."

Jack saved his nickels and he saved his dimes,
He pleaded with his parents a thousand times.

Then one snowy Christmas, a huge box appeared.
Jack tore it open and looked in and cheered,

"A yak! A yak of my very own!
I'm the happiest kid that I've ever known!

I'll take care of him always, though it's quite a big job,
And I'll love my yak and I'll call him Bob."

Jack hugged his parents and he kissed his yak
(Though it felt a little yucchy when Bob kissed him back).

And later that day, in the quiet white snow,
Bob and Jack walked two in a row
And Jack held Bob's leash and felt big inside.
"This is my yak, Bob," said Jack with pride.

And all through that night, asleep in his bed,
Wonderful yak dreams danced in Jack's head.

Now of course responsibilities come with a yak,
But no one could handle them better than Jack.
Since yaks need exercise and room to play,
Jack walked Bob three times each day.

When Bob shed hair all over Jack's room,
Jack swept it up with a special yak broom.
And each day, even if he wasn't in the mood,
Jack prepared a bowl of special yak food.

Then with Mom's help, each Tuesday night,
He gave Bob a bath till his yak hair shone bright.

Jack trained Bob not to jump on the chairs
And not to chase cars or lie down on the stairs.
He taught Bob to "Sit!" and he taught him to "Stay!"
And to fetch the newspaper every day.

And Bob was so smart (if you still need proof),
Jack even taught him to "Give me your hoof!"

Well, as seasons passed with changes of weather,
Bob and Jack grew closer together.
On a spring trip to Grandma's, whose house was quite far,
Bob sat on Jack's lap in the back of the car.

But Grandma, it seems, was a bit of a grouch.
"That yak stays outside! He might ruin my couch!"

So way past his bedtime, into the night,
A boy tiptoed out in the yellow moonlight.
He found his yak and they slept peacefully,
Huddled together beneath an elm tree.

Bob and Jack learned they could trust one another,
That one friend would always be there for the other.
On a hot summer day near the old railroad track,
A bully from town started picking on Jack.
He threw Jack down and called him a name.
Jack called, "Bob, help!" and here Bob came,
Charging and roaring, with angry yak breath,
He just about scared that bully to death.
He chased him home till he slammed his door,
And the bully didn't bother them anymore.

Then there were times that weren't the best,
When sometimes their friendship got put to a test.
One autumn day, Jack came home from school
And found his mom's sweater all covered with drool,
With a button torn off and a hole chewed beneath
That seemed to be made by someone's yak teeth.
"Bad, bad yak!" Jack said to Bob.
"Mom will kill us when she gets home from her job."

"This is trouble!" cried Mom when she got back.
"Oh, please!" Jack cried. "He's not a bad yak!
I know he didn't mean it! Please don't be mad!"

His mother could see Jack was truly sad,
And she understood and said, "It's all right."
But no one could find Bob till late that night
When they saw a wisp of the hair on his head
Sticking out from under the end of Jack's bed.
Then Jack hugged Bob and they both felt better
(And Jack used his allowance to help pay for the sweater).

They stuck together through thin and thick,
Through sun and rain, through well and sick.
One winter when Jack had to stay in bed
With the chicken pox and an ache in his head,
Bob didn't leave him all week long,
He just sat by Jack's bed looking sad and strong.
And every so often he'd give Jack a nuzzle
With his soft, warm, wet, and drooly yak muzzle.

So Jack loved Bob and Bob loved him back
(Though it still was a bit yucchy being kissed by a yak).

By now quite a number of years had passed,
And yaks get older and boys grow up fast,
And the time came for Jack, one autumn day,
To go live at college in a town far away.
The night before, he started to pack,
Then he stopped and sat down alone with his yak.
"I'll be home for vacations, Bob, please don't be mad,
You're the best yak anyone ever had.
I wish you could come, but I won't get my wish,
They just allow hamsters and tropical fish.
No big pets allowed, so you have to stay here."
And Bob just looked puzzled, like the words weren't clear.
Then later, the two friends
slept through the night,
A boy and his yak,
all huddled up tight.

Next morning was busy and by half-past eight
His dad, in the car, called, "Come on, Jack, we're late!"
So with one last hug Jack said, "Be a good yak.
I'll miss you a whole lot until I get back."
And Jack and his parents at just nine o'clock
Drove out of the driveway and off down the block.
Bob sat and watched from in front of the door
Till he couldn't see Jack or the car anymore.

J ack lived at college in a room near the gym
Where schoolmates, not family,
    were living with him.

His days were packed full
            from beginning to end,
There were new friends to meet,
            there was class to attend,

There were lectures and concerts
            and readings and talks,
There were papers and tests, there were picnics and walks,
There was softball and soccer and runs round the track,
But there wasn't much time left for missing a yak.
Now and then Jack thought of Bob, all brown and frizzy,
But it's hard to miss someone when life is so busy.

Meanwhile, at home, Bob spent each day through
Not quite sure where to go, not quite sure what to do.
There were evenings when Jack's dad found strands of yak hair
Shed on the seat of his favorite chair.
And often Bob lay at the foot of Jack's bed
With a chewed-up old slipper tucked under his head.
And sometimes when one of Jack's parents passed by,
They would hear through Jack's wall a big, deep yak sigh.

Well, when Jack came home for his first vacation,
You can imagine Bob's celebration—
He danced and made noises and nuzzled Jack so,
He toppled him over and stepped on his toe.

Jack gave Bob a hug and he patted his head,
And said, "Bob, I'd like you to meet my friend Fred."
(Fred was Jack's school friend, his newest and best,
Jack brought him home as a holiday guest.)
"Give me your hoof, Bob," Fred ordered the yak.
Bob hesitated, then did it for Jack.

Fred stayed all vacation,
        the boys played a lot,
Sometimes with Bob,
        and then sometimes not.

Though Jack still loved Bob, it is fair to mention
That Jack did pay Fred quite a bit more attention.
For much of the week Bob was left on his own,
Then vacation was over, and Bob was alone.

Jack kept himself busy as months passed by
And Bob hardly saw him until July.
Then it was summer and Jack got a job,
So he still didn't have much time for Bob.
Then back to college to work and to play,
With just a quick visit home each holiday.

Well, a year went by, or maybe two,
And one chilly winter Bob caught the flu,
And with Jack's dad, just before vacation,
Bob went to the vet for an examination.
The vet checked him out from his toes to his liver
And Bob sneezed and trembled and let out a shiver.
"This yak," said the vet, "has a terrible cold
And an awful sore throat, and if truth be told,
He's begun to grow old with a weak back and knee,
He's not quite the same yak he used to be.
There's a pet shop downtown, you can buy a yak sweater,
And here are some pills. I hope he feels better."

Jack arrived next day at a quarter to four.
As best he could, Bob ran to the door
And tried to jump up and nuzzle Jack,
But his cold made him weak and he tripped and fell back.
Jack's dad explained that Bob wasn't well—
He was getting older, and that's why he fell.
All through that week, when Bob was with Jack,
He tried his best to be the same old yak,
But he felt so sick, it wasn't much fun.
Then all too soon the week was done.
Jack left on Sunday afternoon.
"You're a good yak," he said.
        "Please get well soon."

Well, Jack finished college and got offered a job
In a faraway city, but he couldn't bring Bob.
(When your life's starting out on a brand-new track,
You can't really bring along your old childhood yak.)
Jack thought of Bob often but still, somehow,
It was more like Bob belonged to Jack's parents now.

Jack lived in an apartment all on his own,
He became a young man, all fully grown,
While Bob, in yak years, reached a hundred and two,
With many things he could no longer do.
He'd try climbing stairs and find that he couldn't,
And often he'd chew on things that he shouldn't.
He was much less alert and no longer as strong,
Sometimes he'd just lie quietly all day long.

Then one night came a phone call from Jack's mom and dad.
Jack could tell from their voices that the news was bad.
His mom said, "You know that Bob hasn't been well."
His dad said, "There's very sad news to tell."
And his father told Jack that Bob had died.
And as big and grown-up as Jack was, he cried.
"We'll all of us miss him," his mom said to Jack.
"We're sorry," said his dad. "He was one great yak."
And that night as Jack lay awake in bed,
So many memories came into his head
Of when Bob was a young yak and Jack was a boy
And each day would bring something new to enjoy.
Now Bob was gone. It just didn't seem real,
And Jack had a new kind of sadness to feel.
He knew that Bob wouldn't be there anymore
And he felt more unhappy than ever before.
Jack whispered out loud so he'd feel less sad,
"You're the best yak anyone ever had."

The same way it feels better after you cry,
A sad thing gets less sad as time passes by.
So before too long, Jack stopped feeling bad
And remembered just the good times that he and Bob had.

Then seasons passed till the night of Halloween,
When he met someone important whose name was Jean.
He met her at a party of a friend called Willy
Where just about everyone was acting silly.

But Jack and Jean sat and had their first talk,
Then, in Halloween moonlight, they went for a walk
And learned they both liked baseball, and poems, and spaghetti.
By the end of the evening, they were friends already.
Through the next months, their feelings grew
(Though they sometimes disagreed, like a lot of people do).
Still, they both began to think that they'd met the right one
Because mostly they were happy and mostly they had fun.

Then one day they knew they were the people for them. . . .
They got married on June 3rd at 11 A.M.

Just two years later it was quite exciting
When their friends received a card with fancy writing:
"Jean and Jack are proud to announce
A new baby girl, 8 pounds 1 ounce.
Her name is Claudette, she was born at noon
On June 21st. Come and see her soon."

IT'S A GIRL!
CLAUDETTE

Well, in what seemed
　　　　like no time at all,
Claudette got a tooth and
　　　　she learned how to crawl.

Then before you knew it,
　　　　she could talk and read

And ride a two-wheeler
　　　　at a pretty good speed.

Not long after that, as he was driving home late,
An idea came to Jack that was immediately great.
It was such an idea that it made his skin buzz,
He just couldn't believe how excellent it was.
By the time he calmed down and tried to
     find his mailbox,
He had driven past his house by fourteen blocks.

Jack had a nifty idea and he knew it,
Now he just had to wait for the right time to do it.

Well, Jack was itchy all through September,
And during October, he longed for November.

When it finally got to be December first,
The next three weeks were the absolute worst,

Till he looked at his calendar and could hardly believe
That at long, long last it was Christmas Eve.

Snow fell softly all during that night
And by morning the trees were heavy and white.

After early breakfast, the whole family
Gathered together round the Christmas tree.
It was time for Claudette to open each box—
First a doll, then a ball, then some bright yellow socks.
Then finally she came to the biggest box yet.

"Go ahead and open it," Jack said to Claudette.
She untied the ribbon, Jack watched as she did—
He felt his heart beat as she opened the lid.
Claudette looked inside and she let out a shout,
And then very slowly . . .

. . . a yak came out.

Claudette was surprised, she wasn't prepared,
For a moment she stopped, looking nervous and scared,
But the yak took a step, and he sniffed Claudette's clothes,
Then Claudette raised her hand, and she patted his nose.
Then the yak stepped in closer and gave her a nuzzle
With his soft, warm, wet, and drooly yak muzzle.
Jack wasn't sure how Claudette would feel,
But she suddenly jumped and let out a squeal.

"Oh, a yak, a yak!" exclaimed Claudette.
"I've always, always wanted a pet!
I'll take care of him forever and he'll never leave,
And I'll love my yak and I'll call him Steve."
Claudette hugged her parents and she kissed her yak
(And she didn't even mind it when Steve kissed her back).

And later that day, in the quiet white snow,
A girl, dad, and yak walked three in a row.
Then Jack stayed behind and watched with pride
As Steve and Claudette walked side by side.

That night as he saw her asleep in her bed,
Jack wondered what dreams were inside Claudette's head.
He kissed her good night and he pulled up the sheet,
Then he patted the yak fast asleep at her feet
And stood still for a moment to remember the scene.
Then he walked down the hallway to be with Jean.
As they turned off the light, Jean said to Jack,
"It's just as if she always wanted a yak.
It's the best Christmas present she ever got.
He'll be a good yak and she'll love him a lot."

That night Jack dreamed of a long time ago
When a boy and his yak took a walk in the snow.

Thanks and appreciation to Rob Weisbach and Deb Futter for their talent and energy, to Matthew Shear and Stuart Applebaum for care beyond the call, to Esther Newberg for her friendship and advocacy, and to Annie Boylan for being, in addition to everything else, a valued first reader.

J.M.

Special thanks to my editors, Rob Weisbach and Deb Futter, to Jenny Smith, and to the kids of Coleridge-Taylor Elementary and The Anchorage School in Kentucky.

C.L.D.